taro

tapioca

grater

chopsticks

teapot

shrimp

sesame oil

bok choy

sesame seeds

carrots

water chestnuts

rice vinegar

coconut milk

sugar

Dim Sum
for Everyone!
Grace Lin

ALFRED A. KNOPF · NEW YORK

THIS IS A BORZOI BOOK PUBLISHED BY ALFRED A. KNOPF

Copyright © 2001 by Grace Lin
All rights reserved under International and Pan-American Copyright
Conventions. Published in the United States of America by Alfred A. Knopf,
a division of Random House, Inc., New York, and simultaneously in Canada
by Random House of Canada Limited, Toronto. Distributed by Random
House, Inc., New York.

KNOPF, BORZOI BOOKS, and the colophon are registered trademarks of Random
House, Inc.

Library of Congress Cataloging-in-Publication Data
Lin, Grace.
Dim sum for everyone! / written and illustrated by Grace Lin. — 1st ed.
        p.   cm.
Summary: A child describes the various little dishes of dim sum that she
and her family enjoy on a visit to a restaurant in Chinatown.
ISBN 0-375-81082-X (trade) — ISBN 0-375-91082-4 (lib. bdg.)
[1. Dim sum—Fiction. 2. Cookery, Chinese—Fiction.] I. Title.
PZ7.L644 Di 2001
[E]—dc21 00-034813

www.randomhouse.com/kids

Printed in Hong Kong
July 2001

10 9 8 7 6 5 4 3 2 1

First Edition

To Lissy, who gives my books out at dim sum restaurants

Dim sum has

many little dishes.

Little dishes on carts.

Little dishes on tables.

Ma-Ma picks
little dishes
of sweet pork buns.

Ba-Ba chooses
little dishes
of fried shrimp.

Jie-Jie wants turnip cakes.

Mei-Mei wants
sweet tofu.

I like little egg tarts.

We eat a little

bit of everything.

Everyone eats a

little bit of everything.

Now there are empty little dishes.

Before dim sum became widespread, *yum cha*, or tea drinking, was an important part of Chinese culture. People would visit teahouses after a hard day's labor and socialize with their family members and friends. Teahouses began to serve small dishes of food for customers to snack on while they drank their tea. These small dishes of dumplings, cakes, and buns were called dim sum. Soon dim sum became more popular than the tea!

Dim sum translates many ways. Some translate it as "touches the heart," from "point" (*dim*) and "heart" (*sum*), because customers point and choose whichever dishes their hearts desire. Others believe dim sum means "little heart," because the dishes served are so small.

The dim sum tradition was brought over to the Western world in the mid-19th century. As well as teahouses, we now have busy dim sum restaurants.

There are many little customs of yum cha and dim sum. For instance, when your teapot is empty, leave it open— it's a sign that you need a new pot. To thank the waiter, tap three fingers on the table. And don't worry if the staff doesn't take away your dirty dishes; after your meal is finished, the waiter will count them to calculate your bill!

Families and friends still crowd into dim sum restaurants all over the world. There, amid the rolling trolleys and the bustling atmosphere, people talk, gossip, and share, just as they did so many years ago.

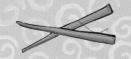

steamed shrimp dumplings
ha gow

crescent dumplings
ham sui gok

stuffed eggplant
yeun ngai guo

coconut pudding cubes
yei tsup go

fried shrimp
tsi ma ha

steamed dumplings
fun gor

sweet tofu
dao fu fai

turnip cakes
lor bak go

rice noodles
cheung fun

sweet pork buns
cha siu bao

steamed meatballs
ngao yuk

thousand-layer cake
tseen tsun go